my science fun

Making Colors Move

Published in the United States of America by Cherry Lake Publishing
Ann Arbor, Michigan
www.cherrylakepublishing.com

Reading Adviser: Marla Conn MS, Ed., Literacy specialist, Read-Ability, Inc.
Book Design: Jennifer Wahi
Illustrator: Jeff Bane

Library of Congress Cataloging-in-Publication Data has been filed and is available at catalog.loc.gov

Printed in the United States of America
Corporate Graphics

About the illustrator: Jeff Bane and his two business partners own a studio along the American River in Folsom, California, home of the 1849 Gold Rush. When Jeff's not sketching or illustrating for clients, he's either swimming or kayaking in the river to relax.

table of contents

Science Notes

Making Colors Move explores surface tension. In this experiment, the reader adds a little soap to a plate of milk. This affects the magnetism of the water molecules within the milk, and the food coloring makes the movement visible.

Do you drink milk? Milk has water and **fat** in it. Whole milk has the most fat.

How often do you drink milk?

Soap makes the fat in milk move.
How can we watch this?

Let's find out!

- Whole milk
- Plate
- Food coloring (red, blue, and yellow)
- Cotton swab
- Dish soap

You will need these things

Pour milk onto the plate. Add two drops of each food coloring. Place the colors on top of each other.

Do you think the colors matter?

Why or why not?

Touch the cotton swab to the food coloring. Watch. Nothing happens.

Put soap on the end of the swab.

Touch it to the food coloring again. Watch.

The colors quickly move around.

The soap **attracts** the fat in the milk. You see the colors moving because the fat is moving.

Will this still happen
without food coloring?

Try it with chocolate milk.
Try it with hot milk. Try it with
glitter instead of food coloring.

Try it with glitter!

Good job. You’re done!
Science is fun!

What new questions do you have?

glossary & index

glossary

attracts (uh-TRAKTS) causing something to move closer or touch

fat (FAT) an oily substance found in some foods

glitter (GLIT-ur) small, shiny objects used to make something pretty

index